Rising Out

M. Azmitia

An imprint of Enslow Publishing

WEST **44** BOOKS™

Please visit our website, www.west44books.com.
For a free color catalog of all our high-quality books,
call toll free 1-800-398-2504.

Cataloging-in-Publication Data

Names: Azmitia, M.
Title: Rising out / M. Azmitia.
Description: New York : West 44, 2022.
Identifiers: ISBN 9781978595439 (pbk.) | ISBN 9781978595422
(library bound) | ISBN 9781978595446 (ebook)
Subjects: LCSH: Poetry, American--21st century. | English poetry. |
Young adult poetry, American. | Poetry, Modern--21st century.
Classification: LCC PS586.3 R575 2022 | DDC 811'.60809282--dc23

First Edition

Published in 2022 by
Enslow Publishing LLC
101 West 23rd Street, Suite #240
New York, NY 10011

Editor: Caitie McAneney
Designer: Seth Hughes

Photo Credits: Cover (people) Monkey Business Images/
Shutterstock.com; (sky) DariaBumblebee/Shutterstock.com.

Printed in the United States of America

CPSIA compliance information: Batch #CS22W44: For further information contact
Enslow Publishing LLC, New York, New York at 1-800-398-2504.

For those who are still digging.

PART ONE

The Plan

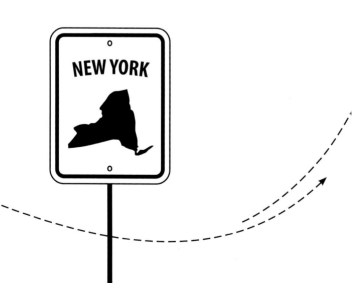

📍

The first time I
saw Eri,

tumbling
onto the grass at
the park near our
homes,

she was a boy
named Maurice.

She screamed as
she fell.

      The Band-Aid
across her nose was
too light.

      Tan on deep, dark
brown skin.

I watched her
blood seep through
the Band-Aid.

Watched it
smear with dirt as
she fell again. But

she screamed

and laughed

and stood up again.

I loved her
before I ever knew
what that meant.

♀

I should not
have been born.

I should have been
a dream forgotten,
set aside.

A split from
this timeline.

A *what if?*

A footnote
in my family
tree.

I was the thing that made
my mother morning-sick.

I was the thing that
nearly killed her
upon arrival.

Or maybe I was
the thing she
sacrificed to stay
alive.

But was it worth it?

I lived, but
there would be
a price.

♀

I grew up knowing
I would need to be

better.

That's the order
of things.

      Isn't it?

Mom does better
than Grandma.

I do better
than her.

We struggle
so the next of us
can step over us,

can go higher.

And *oh*,
did Mom struggle.

♀

My mother's hands
have never been soft.

I've always known them
as strong.

    Hard from the
    work that kept her
    away from me
    for so much of her time.

        Juggling time
        at all her jobs.
        At school.
        At my side.

    Hard from clawing
    through the walls set
    in her path.

    Hard from burying
    her dreams

    so that I could chase
    my own.

Rough when she
held my face
and looked me
in the eye.

    Anaya, she'd say.
    You need to do
    better than me.

♀

She laid out
The Plan
for me

as soon as I could
understand what
she was saying.

• Stay in school.

• Get good grades.

• Don't get in trouble.

• Go to college.

• Get a job.

• Buy a car.

• Buy a house.

    • Then, if,

      and only *if*,

you meet a man

who can
give you something

that you just can't
get on your own:

- Marry him.

- Have a family.

> Be happy in knowing
> that you *won*.

Don't make the same
mistakes I did,
she'd say.

I knew what
she meant.

What she never said.

> *Don't settle for someone*
> *who can't give you*
> *the life you deserve.*

Don't leave your home
for a future so uncertain.

Don't start a family
you're not ready for.

> *Don't make a mistake that*
> *will put your dreams on hold.*

Then she'd pull on
a work shirt.

> One with a
> store logo.
>
> Or one that would
> smell of cleaning
> products when she
> dragged herself home
> in the morning.
>
> Or one that would
> be grease-stained
> and stink of alcohol
> when she got home
> from tending bar.

And she'd leave me,

long after the sky
had darkened.

It was easy, back then.

To be the best.

>   To bring home
>   report cards
>   marked with straight A's.

To be the lead
in every school
play.

>   To be on my best
>   behavior.

To stick to
The Plan.

Before I knew
what she was
asking me

to give up.

♀

When Eri was still Maurice,
I thought we'd
be married
one day.

I never asked,
never said the words
out loud.

But Maurice

    made me laugh.

    Knew about
    The Plan.

Walked me home
to ward off strange men
who'd follow me
when my shape became
that of a woman.

Made me feel safe.

    Had been my best
    friend since I
    was four years old.

Why would I want
anyone else
by my side
when it was finally
time to stop
being alone?

♀

I was 15 years old
when Eri said
she wasn't a boy.

Sitting on the other
end of my couch.

            She had her knees
            pulled tight
            to her chest.

It was late.

Mom was at work.

            Eri flinched
            when she passed
            her phone to me.

            Bracing for impact.

She showed me
an article
on her phone.

            Said the word
            trans

            out loud
            for the first time.

You're the only
one who knows.

She deleted
the history
on her phone

so her dad
would never see.

I should have
been honored
to be the first
to know.

       I was.

       I was also
       terrified.

It was selfish:

I watched my plans
with Maurice

go up in smoke.

       Saw the 16-year-old
       girl in front of me
       when the smoke cleared.

♀

I couldn't marry a woman.

Even if I'd thought about it.

Even if I looked
at both men
and women on TV

with the same
fluttering feeling
in my chest.

It wasn't in
The Plan.

It was okay
for *other people*

to be gay—
to be *bi*—

love is love is love—

but not for me.

♀

How many times
had my mother
been the bad guy?

      How many times
      had I scribbled over
      her face

      in photos of
      my parents?

      Drawn hearts
      around my father's
      face?

How many times
did I say

You're not my mom
anymore

when she dared
to say no to me?

      How many times
      did my father
      get to ride in
      on a white horse

      with a birthday gift,
      an afternoon trip
      to the movies?

How many times
did he get to be
the *good* parent?

       How could I
       let Mom down
       after all she'd done?

I owed her this.

I could learn
to be happy,

just like all
the other women
in my family.

I could learn
to want what
I already had

       and push down
       dreams of
       anything else.

I could be alone—
       always alone—

until I was a success.

Until I was worth
the sacrifice
it took
to get me here.

📍

I could marry
a man who was
kind enough.

Who was
good enough.

Who was

just enough

for me to stick to
The Plan.

       Not messy
       or complicated.

       Who didn't
       start a fire
       in me,

       the way I'd hoped.

But a man who could
keep me safe.

       I could,

       and I would.

That was The Plan.

I looked at the girl
who used to be Maurice—

> Could you call me Eri?

> she asked. Quiet. Afraid.

> I want to try it.

I looked at her

and that same
fluttering feeling

was still there.

> I loved Maurice.

> I would love Eri.

But I couldn't
let that flame
keep burning.

So I buried it.

♀

The first night I knew Eri as Eri,
I couldn't sleep.

I stared at the lights
on my mother's
bedroom ceiling.

> Where she always
> had me sleep
> when Eri stayed over.

I listened to the
rhythm of Eri's snores
from the couch.

I thought about last
Christmas:

> sitting on my living
> room floor.
>
> Surrounded by my
> mother's vinyl records.

Eri had that
faraway look

as she stared at
Donna Summer's face
on the record sleeve.

> *Beautiful, wasn't she,*
> *Maurice?*
> my mother had said.

Had laughed with
a knowing look.

My mom knew nothing.

I should have known then.

I combed through
11 years
of memories.

Searched
for the moment
it should have been
obvious.

There was nothing.

Maurice–

no, *Eri*–

muttered
in her sleep,

the way she always had.

I wondered
how everything
could be so
different

and yet
stay the same.

♀

In the middle of
my senior year,

Eri says
we should
take a road trip.

> We're in her room,
> painting our nails
>
> with the polish she
> keeps hidden
> in her closet.
>
> She'll take it off
> before her dad
> gets home.

You're going
to college
in California.

> There's pride
> in her voice.
> Some sadness, too.
> I'll be at Berkeley for business.
> She has no plans to leave here.

It'll be
like in the movies.

At first
I say no,
but–

I've always
wanted to see
the Pacific Ocean.

I've never
been able

to say no
to her.

📍

I've been wondering
who I am
without The Plan
ever since the
acceptance letter
arrived.

Wondering:
If I peel back
my layers

away from Mom's
watchful eye,

what will I find?

      The letter
      is on my desk.

      Now, The Plan
      is laid out
      in front of me

      in a new way.

I can almost
touch its steps.

Like stones
on a path.

      Hard
      and rough,
      where no flowers grow.

♀

I get ready
for the road trip.

  I spend hours
  tutoring my
  neighbor's kids,

  saving every penny.

  I scribble budgets
  and schedules
  on napkins
  at the dinner table.

  I look up fun and
  interesting landmarks
  on my phone

  on the way
  to school.

I'm a planner.

It's what I do.

  But it's hard to plan
  for the moments

  in between.

For the long
stretches of
golden wheat
fields.

The road
spread out
before us.

The 3,000 miles
of Eri
by my side,

      with nothing
      to hide behind.

Eri knows
who I am
beneath The Plan.

I can tell
from the way
she looks at me:

      like I'm something
      worth looking at.

If she peels back
my layers,

I'm afraid of
what she'll find.

Afraid of what
she'll reveal.

♀

Eri graduated
last June,

but I still see her
every day.

　　She's learning
　　to be a mechanic
　　like her dad.

She's working
in his auto shop,

where everyone
still calls her
Maurice.

Where her dad
calls her *son*

　　and claps a hand
　　on her back
　　instead of
　　hugging her.

I'm the only one
who sees her flinch.

Who sees
the tightness
of her smile

when she laughs along.

♦

We sit outside
the auto shop
on a shaky bench

and plan.

> Look at maps
> online.
>
> Imagine life
> in the far reaches
> of the country.
>
> Imagine
> zig-zagging
>
> up and down
> around its borders.

We decide
to wind down
the east coast

before heading west.

Making stops
along the way.

Making our last
time together last.

📍

Eri's dad watches us
sometimes.

Wipes the
motor oil
off his hands.

Listens as I
do the math:

        the miles,
        the hours,
        the gallons of gas.

He tells Eri:

        Find yourself
        a good woman
        like her.

He winks at me
when he says it.

It's a lie.

Eri's father
once told her:

> Smart women
> like Anaya
> are nothing
> but trouble.
>
> Too hard to
>
> keep
> in
> line.

He was drunk
at the time

and didn't know
that I was on
the other end
of the phone line.

> But for now,
> he winks at Eri
>
> and laughs
>
> and it kills me.

♀

Eri will never
tell her father
who she is.

  She'll always
  flinch a little
  when I reach out
  too fast

  because of him.

  Because of all
  the times he laid
  his hands on her

  for being too loud.

Too *feminine.*

Act *like a man,*
he'd say.

  Too soft.

  Too *much.*

He'll never know
he has a daughter.

Her silence keeps
her safe.

♀

When we're alone,
I call her
by her name.

> Her real one.
> Not the one
> chosen for her.

Eri, what movie
should we watch?

Eri, let me
braid your hair.

Eri, look at this
funny comic.

Oh, Eri? She's my
best friend.

I say this last bit to
an imaginary listener,

just so Eri can
hear me say *she.*

> I watch her relax,
> smile more
> each time I say it

> and I push down
> that fluttering feeling.

♀

Eri loves to touch.

A friendly hand
on my shoulder
as she passes by.

Fingertips
on the back of
my hand
to get my attention.

But only when
we're alone.

She says she
can't do this

with her guy friends
at work.

Can't even do this
with her little brother

without their dad
asking questions.

Saying, *Men don't
do that*.

Because
being a man
is being alone.

But here
in my room,

she holds
my hand.

Touches my hair.

      Tells me
      how soft
      my curls are.

Rests her head
in my lap
as we watch movies.

And I let her

every time.

♀

I touch back.

> Let our fingers
> lace together.
>
> Hold still
> when she tucks
> a stray curl
> behind my ear.
>
> Run my fingers
> through the
> tight coils
> of her hair
>
> when she lies
> against me.

My heart pounds
against my ribs

until I can't hear
anything else.

📍

Every time,
Eri leaves
a trail of
goosebumps

in her wake.

       Every time,
       I'm almost ready
       to come out
       of my skin.

       Every time,
       I feel myself
       being pulled apart.

But I rein myself
back in

every time.

📍

I thought people
had learned to be

quieter

with their hate.

        Thought they only turned their eyes
        and sucked their teeth.

        Complained under
        their breath,

        but let their words
        simmer
        on the backs
        of their tongues.

        Put out
        the fire sparking
        in their palms.

But the spark
has been lit.

It bangs like
gunpowder.

Makes Eri's
fight or flight
kick in.

♀

Gay slurs were shot
at her, like arrows,
like cannonballs,

when she was still
a boy.

       —but she's not even—

Explosive fireworks
crackling from
closed fists

that she almost
didn't
escape.

📍

Eri calls me
as she walks
home from work
late now.

A second job
to save up for
the trip.

She needs
a witness
who will

say her name

if the worst
comes to pass.
She keeps her keys,
jutting and sharp,
between clenched fingers.

It doesn't
stop them.

Doesn't shield her
from the glass bottle
from a passing car

that breaks the skin
above her eyebrow.

The bottle that leaves
her head aching.

Wondering what
gave her away–

The way she walked?

The lilt of
her voice as she
talked to me
on the phone?

The bottle that leaves
her squinting
against the bright
lights in my
bathroom.

The bottle that leaves
her sitting on
the lid of the toilet
while I dab away
the blood.

While I try to joke

and say the scar
will make her
look tough.

But she doesn't

want

to be tough.

More than
anything,

she wants to be
allowed

to be *soft*.

To not
have to pay for it

in fear

and in scars.

♀

A week before
I graduate,

Eri brings me
to her father's shop

early
on a Sunday morning.

> There,
> in the alley
> behind the shop,

> is an old, battered car
> with metallic spots
> of worn-down paint.

> With mismatched
> knobs on the radio.

> With a slightly
> musty smell
> clinging to the
> seats.

Eri has been
rebuilding it
for months
just for me,

getting it ready
for the road
to California.

She calls it
Henrietta.

> *But you can*
> *call her*
> *something else,*
> *if you want.*

> *She's yours,*
> *after all.*

I freeze
in the driver's
seat, my hands

clenched tight
around cracking,
peeling leather.

> *I know*
> *it's not much—*

It's perfect.

> I keep the name.

♀

My mother
wears hospital scrubs
to my graduation.

 She was working
 last night.

 She didn't have time
 to go home
 to shower
 or change.

 She stands,
 embarrassed,
 among well-dressed
 parents.

She says she's sorry–
but I don't care what she wears.

 I know how hard
 she worked
 to earn those scrubs.

 How many nights
 she spent
 cleaning offices,

 stocking shelves,
 serving drinks,
 going to school.

All for the RN
on her work ID.

I'm sweating
in my blue
graduation gown

when she hugs me.

There's a tremble
in her voice
as she says,

*I'm so proud
of you, Anaya.*

My throat
and eyes burn.

I clench
my shaking hands
in the back
of her shirt.

How long
have I waited?

How hard
have I worked?

How much
have I given up

just to hear
those words?

♀

Two weeks later,

I'm sitting
on Eri's bed,

watching her
pack a duffel bag.

        She thinks
        I can't see
        how nervous she is,

        but I can.

The way she
tugs at the coils
of her hair.

The shaky laughter
after everything
she says.

The way she won't
look me
in the eye.

        I see it all.

📍

I bought a dress,
she tells me.

She stares into
her duffel bag

as if
it will answer her.

I look
at the items
spread out
over her bed:

the nail polish
from her closet.

The barrettes,
once hidden
at the bottom
of a drawer.

The eyeliner
that she keeps
stuffed
under her mattress.

I want to know
what it's like
to stop hiding.

When she looks
at me again,

there's fear, yes.

But something
else, too:

an excitement
to be herself,

      like slipping
      into
      her own skin.

It spreads to me,

creeping

like the shallows
at the beach
over sand.

♀

I help Eri pack.

Ask if there's
anything
I can lend her.

       Offer to bring
       my own small,
       basic collection
       of makeup.

Some clothes
I wasn't going
to bring
otherwise.

       Her excitement
       is spreading–
       yes.

       Her smile
       warms me
       until my fingers
       and toes
       tingle.

But somewhere,
in the back
of my mind,

cold and icy,

is the fear.

I've seen
what happens
to women
like Eri.

I've seen
the stats,
the missing
persons photos
of black trans women
like Eri.
The names—

       say her name—

and the parents
in denial.

Searching
for a person
who doesn't
      exist
anymore.

      I'll keep her safe
      and hope
      it's enough.

♀

In the weeks between
graduation
and the road trip,

Mom takes
her first vacation
since before I
was born.

We don't have
the money to
go anywhere, but–

      next summer,
      she promises.

      Next summer.
      Wherever you want.

For now,
we pack a blanket.

A lunchbox.

A flimsy umbrella.

      We squeeze ourselves
      into the back seat
      of the bus.

Brace ourselves
for every bump in the road
on the way from Brooklyn
to the beach.

♀

On the sand,
we huddle together

and share the shade
under our one umbrella.

      Mom plays salsa music
      on her phone
      and hums along,
      quietly.

      Thinks of Cuba,
      the island
      she left
      to find something better
      for me.

She's nearly
drowned out

by the water
lapping at
the shore.

By the sounds
of laughing families.

      I'm sorry.

      She doesn't
      look at me
      when she says it.

She stares
at the water.

Lets it reflect
on her sunglasses.
Hides her eyes.

>   *I wanted better
>   for you, but–*

She picks up
her phone,
opens the
music app.

>   *Now
>   I don't even know
>   what kind of music
>   you like.*

She gives me
the phone, and
I pause–

>   what kind of music
>   *do* I like?

I put it back
down on
the blanket.

Stretch my legs
until the sun
begins to burn
my skin.

◗

Later,

the sun creeping
west across
the sky,

sitting at
the edge
of the sand,

     letting the tide
     tickle my toes,

I realize
the next ocean
I see

might be
the Pacific—

     wider

     and warmer

     and unknown.

♀

Early on
a Sunday morning,

I pack the last
of my things
into the trunk
of the car–

>   *my car.*
>   I almost forget.
>   *Henrietta.*

Mom watches me
from the sidewalk,

pulls her sweater
tight around her.

>   I wonder when
>   I'll step foot
>   in New York
>   again.

We've been
preparing
for this moment
my whole life.

>   Every spelling bee
>   in my bedroom.

>   Every SAT
>   prep class.

Every classmate's
birthday party
invitation

turned down
in favor
of studying.

We knew
this was coming.

Still,

as my mother
hugs me goodbye
for the first time,

I know
we're both

clutching

at each other's backs.

Grasping
for something
familiar

in a world
that seems
new

and scary

and lonely.

PART TWO

The Road

Once Eri and I
cross New York's border,
our first stop
is a lighthouse

on a breezy
Atlantic shoreline.

We'd always meant
to visit it sooner.

We'd watched it through
toy binoculars
since we were kids.

Towering on
some distant shore.

      Eri says
      it's stood through
      wars, through

      people fighting
      to destroy it.

It seems so solid
when I look up
at it.

Something bright
to guide me home.

📍

Henrietta begins
to feel
like her own
person.

> Old
> and grumbling,
> but reliable.

> *Does Henrietta
> need gas?*

> I ask Eri
> on the outskirts
> of Philadelphia.

> *Think we should give
> Henrietta a break?*

> Eri asks me,
> after six hours
> of straight driving.

Henrietta keeps us safe
those first few nights.

Lying back in the
front seats

as we sleep
at rest stops
to save our money.

♀

Henrietta will only play
the music she likes.

She spits out CDs
she doesn't want.

Fills the aux cord
with static
when she thinks
we've chosen
the wrong song.

But Henrietta likes Donna Summer
and Nina Simone.

She and Eri
have that in common.

> *I need you by me,*
> *beside me, to guide me,*
>
> she seems to purr
> along with Eri's voice.

I laugh from
the passenger's
seat.

Watch Eri sway
her shoulders
behind the wheel.

It's easy to forget

how close to home
we still are.

How close
to the people
who keep us
in line.

How much time
is still
ahead of us.

I can't wait.

📍

I like
who I am
when I'm with Eri.

      Free.
      Fun.
      Unafraid.

Not tied down
by what's
expected
of me.

      Two days in,
      I call Mom
      from a rest stop
      in West Virginia
      on a sunny
      afternoon.

Eri's taking a nap
in the back seat.

I speak
quietly.

Make sure
it sounds like
I'm behaving.

Not getting into
any trouble.

When I hang up,
I think of

the first time
I brought home
a grade that started
with an eight.

The way Mom
threw the paper
back at me.

It's not that bad,
I'd tried.

I think of
the sinking feeling
in my gut

when she said,

*You're better
than this,
Anaya.*

⚲

Oh, but
what if I'm not?

What if I'm
not all
she'd hoped
I would be?

      What if this
      was as good
      as it got

      and I'd never
      be better?

How many nights
had I spent
awake,
terrified
by the idea?

By the thought
that I might
be close to

disappointing
her?

I have been
so many things–

a miracle,

a second chance,

something
impossible.

The one who
would finally
make things right.

Everything
except

a person
allowed

to make
mistakes

and learn
from them

and just *be*.

♀

I carry
that sinking
feeling

into the back seat,
pressed up
against
Eri's side.

Forget about
the way my heart
races when our
skin touches.

> Quiet
> my heavy
> breaths.
>
> Sink into
> the guilt
> of relaxing.
>
> Of not working
> toward the
> next thing.

Eri stirs
from sleep.

Reaches for me.

Doesn't ask
questions.

📍

I like
who Eri is
when she's
with me.

I saw it
back home.

Hidden away
behind the walls
of my room.

I see it now,
tenfold.

The way
her shoulders
finally relax

as we wander through
historical towns in
Virginia.

The way she
smiles
and laughs
so freely.

The way she
can touch
and be touched

without fear.

Eri is
so beautiful
when she's
not afraid.

I think about
the end of
this trip,
two weeks from now.

When I stay
in California

and she boards
a plane
back to the
East Coast.

I imagine
all of her
progress

rewinding,
like my mom's old
videotapes
that we watched
as kids.

I can't stand
the thought.

I hope she likes
who she is

with or without me.

When it's my
turn to drive,

Eri reads.

> Short stories.
> Classic novels.
> Poetry.
>
> Fiction,
> history,
> biographies.
> Art. Science.

I never knew
she read
so much.

Never knew
she wanted to.

> *I never had*
> *the time,*
>
she says
when I ask.

She reads over breakfast
at a North Carolina diner.

> *Time,*
> she said.
>
> I want to give her
> all of mine.

◆

We take local roads
for the rest of the day.

A slice of a life
we'll never have.

>   Eri follows
>   a handwritten sign
>   pointing us toward
>   a yard sale.

I like the way
her eyes light up

>   at every vinyl
>   record, every
>   funky lamp.

She finds more books—
touches soft, worn
bindings with
something like awe.

>   I stand back, push down
>   that warm feeling in my chest.
>   Watch her charm the owners.

Funny, loud, unashamed.
In fitted clothes she wouldn't
dare wear at home.

>   I watch her throw
>   her head back
>   and laugh, curls bouncing.

♀

Eri always
reads to me
after dinner.

       In the car,
       front seats tilted back.

Or when we
treat ourselves
to musty
roadside hotels.

While we lie
back on separate
beds.

       I lose count
       of the nights
       I fall asleep

to the sound
of her voice.

To the light
turning of pages.

To the rhythm
of the words
as she reads.

◉

The first time
Eri wears
the sundress,

we pick peaches
in North Carolina.

I'm flipping
through one of
her books

      when she
      creeps out
      of the
      motel bathroom.

      Tugging
      the hem
      down to
      her knees.

I drop the book.

      Ready?
      she asks.

I nod,
reaching
blindly
for the car keys.

📍

She fidgets
with the dress
at every moment.

       Pulls at the
       hem.

       Adjusts
       the straps.

       Holds her
       arm in front
       of herself.

       Hides the way
       the yellow fabric
       stretches across
       her chest.

I keep my
eyes on
the road.

Listen closely
to the GPS.

Unsure if
I should say
something,

anything.

You look pretty,
I say.

She doesn't
answer. Instead
she tightens
the knot

on the red
bandanna
holding back
her corkscrew
curls.

I meant it.

♀

Later,

in between
the quiet rows
of peach trees,

I watch her
reach for ripe
fruit near the top.

She cries out as
three more
peaches fall,

then throws
her head back
and laughs.

I'm rooted
to the spot,

half-full bag
of peaches
dangling from
my fingers.

Seeing her,
bathed in
sunlight:

soft yellow
strap, digging
into dark brown
skin.

Curls bouncing
under the
bandanna.

Framed by
soft, swaying
leaves and
fuzzy stone fruit.

Her smile–
was it always
this bright?

♀

The sight is
new,

in some ways.

And yet,
so achingly
familiar

in others.

This is Eri:

the version of
her

I've always
known,

come to life
in stunning
color.

Finally
here,

for the world
to see.

♀

We eat peaches
for days.

     Always reaching
     for the bag
     in the back seat.

     Feeling for
     fuzzy skin.

We find
a motel
with a tiny
kitchenette.

     Look up how-to
     videos on our phones
     about making peach cobbler.

     Look up what a cobbler
     even *is*.

We try
to figure out
how to make
jam, but

get lost
in the details.

📍

We find ourselves
eating peaches
in the sun.

South Carolina
sees us

lying
on the pale sands
of Myrtle Beach

with nothing
but peaches
and water
bottles

to keep us
going.

We don't need
anything else.

Just sun and

sand collecting
on juice-sticky
fingers–

and each other.

♀

I wear cargo
pants rolled
to my knees

and a floppy
sunhat I picked
up at a rest
stop on Route 1.

> Eri wears denim
> shorts and
> a crop top

> that she found
> at another
> yard sale
> this morning

> and a pair
> of sandals
> she borrowed
> from me.

> Ones I know
> I'll let her keep.

She jokes
about burying me
in the sand

if I fall asleep.

♀

We stay
until the sky
runs pink

with the day's
end

and our skin
prickles
with sun.

On our way
back to
Henrietta,

Eri stops me
for a selfie.

One long,
strong arm
around my
shoulder.

Cracks a joke
about beaches
back home, littered
with cigarette butts.

We laugh,
framed
by the SkyWheel.

📍

Georgia
finds us

leaning over
railings on
walkways in
Magnolia Springs.

> I watch turtles
> paddle lazily
>
> through
> crystal-clear
> water, tinted
> blue in the sun.
>
> Blooming with green.
>
> Still and quiet.

Eri read about
natural springs
this morning.

She points out
the dark
spots where
water

flows from
underground.

As she talks,

her voice is bright
with the joy
of sharing
what she knows.

I think about
her time in
school.

How she did
well enough
to pass,

to graduate,

but never
put in the time
that I did.

Too busy
balancing

classes and
working
in her dad's shop

to bother.

♀

Still,

I think,

as she uses
her hands to
teach me new things—

about *aquifers*
and *water tables*—

she's smarter
than she ever
let on.

   It's like a sponge,

   she says.

   Squeezing out water
   from below.

She smiles as
understanding
flickers in
my eyes.

♀

Later, I gasp
at the first
alligator I've
ever seen.

Reach for Eri's arm
and squeeze as she laughs.

> What if alligators
> were red?
> I joke.

They'd starve,
she tells me.

Blending in
helps them survive.
Standing out would
ruin their chances.

Then she takes my hand
and pulls me away.

> I think about
> how she could
> have bested me
> in school

> with half the effort,
> if she'd been
> given the chance.

That night,
we lay
a blanket over
Henrietta's hood.

Sit and look up
at the stars

we could
never see
back home.

      Eri,
      always needing
      to touch,

      reaches
      for my hand
      again.

Here, lit by
nothing but
stars,

I imagine
we can finally
be who we are.

      Covered by
      darkness

      where the sun
      can't see.

♀

I saw Orion
last night
so clearly.

      Or was it
      the night before?

I lose track
of the days
on the road.

      At lonely rest stops
      where we take turns sleeping.

      In musty motel rooms
      with neon signs
      buzzing outside.

I lose track
of the miles
stretched out
behind us.

      Echoing with
      our laughter.

I lose track
of the steps
of The Plan

      and of the thought
      that I can never
      stop working.

♀

I haven't
thought about

The Plan

in what feels
like forever.

> Instead, I'm singing
> songs that make
> me forget.

> Telling jokes
> I would never dare
> tell at home.

> Reading books
> that I enjoy.

> That aren't for school.

> That aren't a step
> to get ahead.

I'm living
for myself,

and myself alone,

in a way I've
always been
afraid to.

📍

I could never
have imagined

what it would
feel like

to stop
worrying.

       To not ask
       whether each
       moment,

       each action,

       each step and
       breath I take,

is guiding me
toward
The Plan—

       or leading
       me
       the wrong way.

Instead,
a day
is just a day

and not a path
to tomorrow.

📍

The rainy days that follow
find us inside more.

     Wipers squeaking
     across Henrietta's windshield.

     Fighting off
     the downpour.

Eri reads to me
from the
passenger's seat.

     About plantations.

     About people
     bought and sold

     in the name of a
     growing South.

I glance at
green signs
guiding us to
those same places

as we cross the border
into Alabama.

     I imagine
     huge estates
     built by unsung labor.

Eri goes quiet.

♀

I keep driving.

That night,
rain pelts against
our motel windows.

Eri is reading
again as I
towel-dry my
deep brown curls.

> From her phone
> on the table,

> Billie Holiday sings
> to a blue moon.

Eri puts down
her book.

Stands.

Reaches one
hand out to me.

> I take it,

> let her
> pull me closer.

◉

I never went
to a school
dance.

            Never bothered
            with dates.

Never bothered
with anything

that wasn't

studying and
working and
planning.

            Eri doesn't
            seem to mind
            my two left
            feet

            as we shuffle across
            the motel carpet.

She's patient and
doesn't laugh

when I get
the steps wrong.

Guides me with
a hand on
my back

as our sundresses
sway
together.

As the song
changes.

As the rain
washes away

our secrets.

♀

Sometimes
Henrietta will
sputter. Vibrate
with the effort
of moving.

        Eri pulls into
        a rest stop,

        pops the hood
        open. Tinkers

        with parts I only
        sort of understand.

I've never
told Eri
how much I
enjoy watching
her work.

        The strength
        she shows

        when she wrinkles
        her brow.

        When she scans
        the engine for
        what could be wrong.

♀

I've never told
Eri how my skin
prickled with warmth

when I'd see her
after work
at her dad's shop:

       in stained
       coveralls and
       a smear of grease
       on her cheek.

Even now,
I turn away.

Let her work
with the tinny
sounds of Donna
Summer

playing from
her phone on
Henrietta's roof.

There's no echo.

No ceilings
or walls for
the notes to
bounce on.

I can almost
watch them

drift out over
the Alabama River.

*When you find
the perfect love,
let it fill you up,*

Eri sings along,
quietly.

♀

Eri's wearing
shorts, with her
long, strong legs

straining as she
leans over
Henrietta.

A loose, flowing
graphic tee
printed with bees

droops to reveal
her collarbone.

      The end is
      tied and knotted
      to keep it from

      snagging on
      the inner workings
      of the engine.

📍

Even before
this trip,

even back home,

I loved the two
sides of her–

      loved how she
      could be firm

      and broad
      and strong

      in a way I
      never was,

      when she
      needed to be.

Loved when she
could be soft

and kind
and open

when she was
alone with me.

📍

Now,
as I watch her
hum under
the hood.

As she makes
her way back
to the driver's
seat.

As she turns
the key in
the ignition.

As she shouts
with a smile
when Henrietta
purrs without
a sputter–

I know
it was wrong

for me to see her

as two people.

To put the different
parts of her
in boxes

as if they
could be separated.

Because all of it
was her.

       She was always
       there.

I see
all the parts
of her

together now,
brilliant
and beautiful.

As she closes
the hood and,
smiling,

waves for me
to hop back
into the passenger's
seat,

       I see all of her.

       And fear curls
       in my gut
       as I realize

       just how badly

       I want her even more.

♀

Eri asks me
to help her
with her
eyeliner.

She's wearing
a new dress,
just because.

Navy blue
with a pink
floral print.

She only tugs
at the hem
a few times.

With no one else
who knew her
before,

who still calls her
Maurice,

she's free
to be herself.

♀

I remind myself
that that's a good
thing.

As I watch her
eyelids flutter
while I drag
the pencil over
her lash line.

As I see
her curls frizz
with the wet,
sticky air.

As I catch
the scent
of manuka honey
soap on her skin.

It's hard
not to lean
in closer.

To push down
those feelings

when every
part of her

draws me in.

It's harder, still,

when she feels
free to do this:

    to step outside
    in her new
    dress.

    In eyeliner and
    in sandals that
    used to be mine.

    In half-braided
    hair that I
    styled for her.

When she's
by my side
at every moment.

    Finally able
    to laugh
    and act freely.

It's harder
to forget
those feelings

    when she is
    herself:

    truly
    and fully.

📍

The Southern coast
drifts by

      in a blur of
      ocean breezes.

The air
feels different
as we head northwest
into the mountains of
Mississippi.

Appalachia.

On our way to
Memphis, Tennessee.

      The air is
      thicker, stickier.
      Cicadas screech
      at night

      as we unfold
      ourselves from
      Henrietta.

It's small,
at first.

A motel clerk
refusing
to look Eri
in the eye.

Addressing me
as if I were
alone.

But as we drive
to places where

wrath

is something
reserved for God,

it still seems
to seep
into every moment
of Eri's life.

As if she's
being punished
for existing.

♀

In a
laundromat,

as I show her
how to wash

her new,
delicate clothes—

a mumbled
comment

about what a man
should
and should not
wear.

There's a certain
feeling

when a hateful word
is hurled
at you.

A chill of fear
splashing across
the skin.

A hot, sinking
feeling
in the gut.

Embarrassment
for existing.

I feel it
wash over me
in that moment.

As I swallow
it down

and curl
my fists
around a
dirty T-shirt.

Hoping
against all hope

that Eri
didn't hear.

But she goes
quiet, after,

and I know
she did.

♀

I stand
in the motel
parking lot

and call my mom
while Eri
books a room.

      Mom asks
      how it's going.

      If I'm having fun
      and staying safe.

      If I'm getting
      ahead of my
      reading for college.

      (I'm not.)

She asks me
for photos.

I pause.

♀

I think about
the photo I took
of Eri at Myrtle Beach.

       The sun
       reflecting the
       highlight on
       the high points of
       her cheekbones.

       Stunning
       and powerful.

       With me as
       the only one
       trusted to
       witness it.

I tell Mom
that I've been
having fun

and forgetting
to take photos.

📍

    The lie
    turns sour
    in my gut

as I glance
at my phone.

At the photo
on my
lock screen:

    Eri and I
    framed by
    the SkyWheel.

    My favorite photo
    from this trip
    so far.

Beautiful
and joyful
and treasured.

    Yet
    no one but Eri
    will share it
    with me.

◉

There's only
one bed,
Eri tells me

as she tosses
an old-fashioned
room key
my way.

I don't catch it.

I scoop it up
from the
ground.

I barely sleep
that night.

Too busy
inching closer
to the edge
of the bed.

We slept so close
in the car, but
a bed feels different.

Eri doesn't
move once
she's asleep,

but her quiet
snoring feels
like a siren
in my ear.

♀

I need
the distance.

Need to
force back
thoughts of what
it would be like

to sleep
close to her,
always.

      To hear the way
      she hums as
      she rolls over

      in the middle
      of the night.

To have her always
within arm's
reach.

♀

I need
to stop
imagining

waking up
next to her
as a habit.

Having her
look at me

in that way she does.

Like I'm
worth something.

Like she enjoys
looking at me.

It feels silly,
like something
out of a
cheesy romance novel.

Like one of those
mournful songs
written by sad,
lonely teens

with no other
worries,

no other problems.

But in
that moment,

I understand them,

> and I feel
> the weight
> of that
> understanding.

I have to
move closer
to the edge
of the bed.

> Have to
> clench my fists
>
> and fight
> the need
>
> to reach out
> to her
>
> in the safety
> of scratchy
> motel bedsheets.

Have to
stay awake

and keep
from dreaming.

♥

I never told Eri
or Mom.

Never even
admitted it
to myself,
really.

All those months
ago, filling out
college applications.

Crossing my fingers
for California.

3,000 miles
between home
and me.

3,000 miles
between Mom
and me.

3,000 miles
between

Eri

and me.

I needed
to leave.

◉

Maybe
there were
other reasons,

     but the need
     to start over
     far from Eri

     was still there.

The need
to put distance
between

myself

and the life
I wanted

but

could never
have.

     The fear
     that she would

     forget about me.

The hope
that I
would do
the same.

◉

Eri and I
split at the
door of a
grocery store.

Hunting
for snacks
for the road.

I'm reaching
for a box on
the top shelf.

My fingertips
just barely touch
the box

when it happens.

When an
unfamiliar voice
says,

*Let me get that
for you.*

When an
unfamiliar hand

touches down
on the small
of my back
and squeezes.

I fight
the instinct
to flinch,
to swing.

> That cold,
> creeping feeling
> is back.

> Reminds me of
> men back home,

> following me
> after school.

> Taking photos
> of me
> on the subway.

> Touching
> as if they
> had any right.

This man,
young and handsome
as he is,
still stands too close.

Makes his fingers
brush against mine
as he hands me
the box.

Lets his touch
drag along my wrist.

Then, as expected,
come the
questions.

> *What's your
> name?*
>
> *How old
> are you?*
>
> *(This question
> almost
> never matters.)*
>
> *Where are
> you from?*
>
> *Are you
> free later?*
>
> *Can I
> call you?*

I do my best
to not answer
without seeming
rude.

> Never sure
> of how he'll
> react if
> I just say no.

At least
I manage

to move
away from
his hand.

Clutch
my basket
in front of me.

       Put some space
       between us.

Try to
bore him
until he leaves.

       But he doesn't leave.

I step back
when he reaches
for my
shoulder, hard.

       A laugh.

       Don't be
       like that,
       sweetheart.

As if
sensing
my distress,

Eri appears
at the end
of the aisle.

> Tilts her head
> when she sees me—
>
> *Are you okay?*
>
> she asks.
>
> *Do you need help?*

I try to
nod, just
a bit.

> She's lovely
> today—
>
> made up,
> imposing,
> powerful
>
> as she makes
> her way
> toward me.

She puts one hand
on my elbow.

Makes the man
trail off.

  Ready to go?

  she asks.

It's not
the first time
she's done this–

  always stepping in
  when she was still
  Maurice.

  Pretending to be
  my boyfriend.

  Because some men
  respect another
  man's claim

  more than a
  woman's will.

It doesn't
work the same
way, this time.

◉

Instead, the man
steps away.

Shows his teeth
when he glares.

So that's
what you like?

The sweet note
in his voice

has soured,
acidic as he
spits the
words out.

He wipes
the hand that
touched me
on his shirt,

as if brushing
a stain away.

Disgusting.

He leaves me
alone, but as
Eri freezes
beside me,

I have to wonder
at what cost.

◉

Eri is quiet
as she drives
back to the motel.

She keeps her
hands at ten and
two. Doesn't

hum along with
the music on
the radio. Doesn't

drum her fingers
on the steering
wheel.

I curl up,
silent, in the
passenger's seat.

Watch the road
blur by.

♀

The air conditioner
in the motel room
is broken.

     The open window
     does nothing
     but let in more
     warm, thick air.

Still,
I turn the water
in the shower
as hot as
I can stand.

     Until steam
     seems to cling
     to my skin.

     I scrub away
     at the parts that man
     had touched until

     my skin is
     deep pink and
     raw.

♀

Eri wears
long sleep pants
despite the heat.

> Rolls long
> sleeves to
> her elbows.

There's a
board game
laid out on
the desk.

> A thrift store
> find, with
>
> different-sized
> coins taking
> the place of
> missing pieces.

We play for
a few minutes

before she says it:

> *Maybe this
> was a bad idea.*

She waves
a hand at the
pile of her
clothes from
earlier today.

At the shared
makeup bag

on the table
between our beds.

At her painted
nails.

*Maybe I should
tone it down.*

I can't
really bring
myself to
answer her.

Can't make
myself tell her

to stop
being herself.

Can't make
myself tell her

to stop
being safe,
either.

Mostly
I start
to wonder

if she's right,

but for
different reasons.

      Maybe this
      was a bad idea.

Maybe it
would have been
better

to stick to
The Plan.

      To say no
      to this trip.

      To say no
      to spending
      this much time
      with Eri,

      making it hard
      to think clearly.

To say no
to dragging her
through these
towns where

we're clearly
not welcome

       and we can't
       even

       figure out
       why anymore.

If it's because
of our black
and brown
skin

or the way
we hold hands–

       we're not even–

or the way
Eri dares
to not hide.

       How is it
       even possible

       to be hated

       for so many
       different reasons?

♀

We never make it
to Memphis.

We drive faster–
south again–
leaving the mountains
behind us.

The distance
seems to stretch
out so much
slower.

Time
passes slow like
thick syrup.

      Henrietta
      rolls us out
      further west.

As I drive,
I imagine

changing course,
coming up with
a new plan,
a new path.

      But we had
      a plan,
      a schedule.

A need to get
to California
before school starts.

A seat
on a flight
heading back home

with Eri's
name on it.

Lives
to get back to.

A need
to be
responsible.

There's no time.

We keep going.

📍

Just past the border
into Louisiana,
we have dinner
at a roadside diner

that feels
like a bar.

      Hours of
      quiet

      bleed into Eri's
      need to touch.

She holds
my hand from
across the table.

Pulses her grip
until I squeeze
back.

      Eri's hair
      is loosed from
      the braids.

      Held back by
      borrowed barrettes.

📍

A waitress
approaches from
behind Eri.

Pats her apron
and doesn't look
up as she greets
us.

>Hey, *ladies,*

>she says.

>Voice light,
>lilting.

When she
looks up

and sees Eri,
she frowns.

>*Sorry, sir.*

It should
be nothing–

>Eri has heard
>worse, held her
>head up high

>through worse.

But it's been
hard, these days,

a series of
small, cruel
comments.

Weighing
her down with
each word.

I don't
know what to say
to make it better.

              I'm not sure
              if I ever will.

              Suddenly
              the firm, sure
              tone

              the waitress
              uses seems
              pointed.

Meant to sting.

📍

Eri's not
wearing a dress,
but

in a small
town like this,

it may not matter.

      A feminine sandal.

A pair of shorts
a few inches
too high.

Too tight.

      A shirt that
      rides up as
      Eri leans
      forward

      to hear
      what I'm saying.

Painted nails and

      a floral barrette.

As the night
goes on,

the waitress
seems intent
on making
a point.

      Sir.
      Sir.
      Sir.

      To Eri.

Miss.
Miss.
Miss.

To me.

      Maybe she
      doesn't mean
      for it to seem

      as forceful
      as it does.

It doesn't matter.

📍

No one
but me

would be able
to see:

      the way
      Eri begins

      to shrink in
      on herself.

The way
her laughter

gets quieter
and smaller.

      The way she
      tries so hard

      to take up
      as little space
      as she can.

Tries
to not make
a sound.

📍

She stops
reaching for me.

Keeps her
hands folded
in her lap.

      I search
      for the right
      words.

      They never come.

♀

After meals
eaten in silence,

Eri keeps
her head down
as she shuffles
back to Henrietta.

      I hang back,
      grip the sink
      in the bathroom

      and take
      deep breaths.

I could have
said something.

Maybe I
should have,
but

      would it help?

      Would Eri want
      the extra
      attention?

      Or was it better
      to let her
      deal in private?

♀

When I walk out,

I'm cornered

     by a tall,

     broad man

with whiskey
on his breath.

     As if
     he could sense
     my hopeless
     feelings.

     As if he
     knew I'd be
     a weak target.

I feel my blood
begin to race.

     My eyes dart
     around me

     for an escape route

     before he ever
     says a word.

📍

I have to
wonder what
did it
this time.

Maybe
I was too
obvious

in the way
I reached
for Eri.

Maybe it was

the way
I looked
at her.

Eri is
alone
in the parking lot.

Maybe
I put us
in danger

because I
couldn't keep
my feelings
in check.

♀

My skin
crawls and

I feel bile
rise in
my throat

as he leans in.

      As he asks
      if I need
      a *real man.*

If he's drunk
and slow,

maybe I can
get past him–

      I glance
      at a woman
      coming out
      of the bathroom.

She's older,

with deep
brown skin.

Hair graying
at her temples

and a kind face.

> A face like
> I always
> imagined
> Eri's mom
> would have.

> I plead with
> my eyes.

Without
a second thought–

> *There you are,*

> she says.

> *We're going
> to be late.*

She grabs my arm

and pulls me away.

📍

I don't tell
Eri
about what
happened.

       I don't
       add my own
       baggage
       to hers.

In the days
that follow,

Eri won't
be touched.

       Will flinch
       when I reach
       out to her.

She pulls
her old clothes

from the bottom
of her bag–

       baggy jeans
       that cover
       shaven legs.

Loose hoodies
that hide
the planes
of her chest.

Her hair
tied into
a tight,
unforgiving bun.

       She sweats in
       the summer
       heat.

       Brushes off
       all of my
       concerns

       when I ask
       if she's sure.

If she wants
to go back

and change.

She insists
she's fine
every time.

       Climbs into
       Henrietta.

♀

I wish
she'd tell me
what she needs.

What it will
take for her
to feel safe.

If she even
knows the answer.

Instead,
I see her
get dressed.

School
her face into
something
that passes–

for *okay*.

For masculine.
For unafraid.

The layers cover up
all the parts of her
that shine.

The parts of her
I've loved
for years
and years.

♀

I'll never know
what it's like.

       I could
       point out
       the parts of me
       that might *seem*
       masculine too,

and tell her
that they don't
change anything.

       Like the way
       I need to take
       a razor
       to my chin
       twice a week.

Like the way
I need to pull
thick, black
hairs from
my upper lip.

       These things
       don't make me
       less of a woman.

I could tell Eri
that even though

I've decided
I will never bear
a child,
despite the blood
I spill
every month–

       I'm still
       a woman.

But the words
die on
my tongue
every time.

       I'm still
       a woman,
       yes, but–

no one
has ever
looked at me
and thought

I was
anything else.

♀

New Orleans was
supposed to be
the best part

of the road trip.

An afternoon
strolling
through
the French Quarter.

An evening
spent taking in

the sights and
sounds of
Bourbon Street.

Ghost walks
that would
leave us with

more laughter
than fear.

Parks and
museums and
venues

in memory of
Eri's favorite
jazz artists.

> With her
> by my side,

> well-read
> and informed.

> Guiding me
> through the
> city's
> history.

I'd been
looking forward
to so much.

Had hoped
for so much.

So ready
to share it
with Eri.

But she's
still quiet.

Still
overdressed.

Still hesitates
to leave the
motel room.

Still insists we
stay inside
today

and the
next day.

I know
I should
say something,

but I wouldn't
even know
how to start.

How to
tell her
I understand

when I never
really will.

♀

My mind
wanders back

to The Plan.

To the thought
that maybe

I've made
a mistake.

> That Eri
> wouldn't feel
> this way

> if I'd worked
> harder
> to protect her.

If she was
with someone

who could
make her feel
less alone.

If I'd done
my job
and stuck to
The Plan−

> she might have
> someone stronger
> at her side.

♀

I wonder
if Eri
has regrets

about coming
all this way
with me.

      If she wishes
      she were here

      with someone
      else.

I pretend
to sleep
as she drives,

and we never
talk about it.

      We suffer
      quietly

      and keep
      moving west.

📍

We meant
to visit
the Space Center
in Houston.

    We'd made plans
    while Eri
    talked in

    fast,
    excited
    sentences.

But we barely
make it past
breakfast.

In the diner
parking lot,

Eri
collapses.

♀

Fear spikes
cold and sharp
in my chest

    when I
    rush to her,

    put my hands
    on her face,

    feel her
    overheated
    skin under
    my palms.

I struggle
to pull her
into the backseat.

    Start Henrietta
    with shaking
    hands.

Turn on
the air conditioner
full blast.

Listen to it
rattle and
hope it stays on.

Turn the vents
toward Eri.

Peel off
as many of
Eri's layers
as I can.

Grab a bottle
of water
from under
the seat.

Pour it out
over her hair.

Call her name
until her eyes
begin to flutter
open.

♀

She's burning
up, still,
when she opens
her eyes.

I tilt
another bottle
of water
toward her lips.

      I try to
      keep calm.

      Make her believe
      that I know
      what I'm doing.

      That I can
      keep her safe.

Take care
of her

like she's always
done for me.

      She swears
      she's fine,

      just needs
      to rest,

      just needs
      a minute.

◉

I wonder
if she knows

how scared I was
of losing her.

At the motel,

I guide her
toward a cool
shower.

Hover outside
the bathroom door.

Listen for
anything
going wrong.

Twist my hands
until welts form
on my skin.

      Even when
      she's cooled down,

      resting,

      drinking water,

      I can't stop
      worrying.

I press
cool cloths
to her skin.

Fetch glass
after glass
of water,

> even though
> she insists
> she can do it
> herself.

I sit by
her bed

and read aloud
to her.

> I'm not
> as good at it
> as she is.

I know I can't
pull her into

the story
like she does
for me.

Can't carry her
to fantasy worlds

where people can
be dragon kings and

sorcerers and

witches.

       But she listens
       anyway,

       keeps her eyes
       on me.

When she falls
asleep,

I watch
every moment

for the steady
rise and fall
of her chest.

Counting
and waiting.

♀

I walk down
the hall
for ice,

just to keep
my hands busy.

Rest my forehead
against the cool
surface of

the machine
as the bucket fills up.

It's barely
noon, but

already
a deeply tired
feeling

creeps into
my bones.

I think about
what will happen

at the end
of August.

When Eri is
3,000 miles away–
out of reach,
of my care.

♀

As Eri sleeps,
I hold her hand.

I think about
all the stories

where people
like us

die.

Star-crossed

and tragic.

Punished
for our crimes.

      For sharing
      soft moments,

      twining
      our fingers
      together–

      loving.

As if
we have
any right.

I have
to wonder
if there could ever

be something
more.

I have to hope
there's

something more.

♀

I sleep
next to Eri,

if only
to remind myself
that she's
still here

with me.

      To listen for
      the steady sounds

      of her snores.

Feel her shift
on the mattress,

pull all
the blankets
to herself.

      Just to know
      that she's
      there.

♀
When I
wake up,

Eri is seated
on the other bed.

Surrounded
by the books

that have been
piling up
in Henrietta's trunk.

Over a dozen
spread out
on the bed.

She bites at
her fingernails

as she flips
the pages.

Dog-ears the
corners, then
reaches for
the next one.

She mumbles,
but I can't
make out
the words.

◐

I pretend
to sleep for
a while longer.

Give her
a quiet moment
alone.

She's wearing
the yellow dress,

crumpled up
high on her legs

while she focuses
on her reading.

       She knows
       I'm awake.

She begins
to read aloud.

All stories
of women

who refused
to be silent.

       Refused
       to be ignored.

Refused
to hide
and not be seen
as themselves.

In courtrooms,

    where people laughed
    and called them
    "man-monsters."

In doctor's
offices,

    deprived
    of care

    but not deprived
    of a voice.

On stages
and screens
and on paper.

    On front seats
    of buses.

Women who sat
in front of
pianos in
1963 Mississippi.

On computer
screens,

      makeup in hand.

On tennis courts
and in boxing
rings.

      Throwing
      the first brick

      when no one
      would listen.

None of them hid,

Eri tells me.

She smooths down
her dress, brushes
back her hair.

I can see
her hands shaking.

They wouldn't hide,
Eri says.

So *why should* I?

In a world
that wants her

to shrink down
who she is,

to be *less,*

there's no
better way
to rebel

than to be *more.*

♀

We make it
to the Space Center.

> Eri's grip
> on my hand
> is so tight.

> Sweat gathers
> in both our palms.

But we make
our way through.

> We talk about
> life on Mars.

Eri tells me
it's red because
of iron.

> Tells me
> about its
> wide valleys.

Touches
a piece of it
with me.

> Both of us
> too lost in space

> to care about
> the world below.

♥

That night,
as I emerge
from the bathroom,

toothbrush
in hand,

    Eri pulls aside
    the blankets on
    her bed
    for me.

    I lie down
    next to her.

I think about
how brave
she was today.

    How strong
    she's always been.

    How strong
    and how soft.

    How lovely
    and how powerful.

How much
greater she is

than the sum
of her parts.

♀

I think again
about those stories

where people
like us
die,

and I think
there must be

something more.

A home,
maybe.

Eri's laughter
and warmth
and strength.

The exploding
colors of
a garden,

full of life—

and maybe,

just *maybe*,

time.

Together.

📍

Eri is so brave.

> She makes me
> want to be more.

Makes me want
to fight for
the happy endings
we deserve.

I turn to her
in the dark.

> *Eri.*

Reach my hand
to her.

Invite her
to move closer,
if she'll have me.

Anaya.

It feels
like a dam
breaking:

> the bliss
> of having her
> reach right back.

In a new way, this time.
This is love.

♀

In the morning,
as Eri snores
beside me,

I make changes
to The Plan.

- Stay in school

    and learn
    something
    about myself.

- Make friends

    who make
    me feel like
    part of something
    bigger
    than myself.

- Get good grades.

    Challenge myself
    and honor
    the work I do.

- Don't get in trouble,

    unless it's for
    something worth
    fighting for.

- Get a job

    that gives me
    a sense of purpose.
    That makes people
    like us
    feel safe.

- ~~Buy a car.~~
- Take care of Henrietta.

- Buy a house

    to share with Eri.

    To build a life
    where we don't
    have to hide.

    To surround
    ourselves
    with people
    who nurture us.

    A place
    where we can

    help each other
    grow.

- Change The Plan
  as I change, too.

    Let the change
    happen.

174

📍

The air
feels lighter

as we keep
heading west,

      but that may
      just be me.

Lighter.
Not weighed down

      with a legacy
      I never chose.

Not burdened.

      Having someone
      to help me carry
      it all.

There's work
to be done,
still.

      Our work is
      never over,

but there's
hope for
something better.

Something more.

♀

I'd forgotten
what it means

　　　to want.

　　　To feel
　　　my heart
　　　leap

　　　and reach
　　　for something
　　　all on its own.

Not chasing
something chosen
for me.

Not dragging along
the sour taste of guilt.

Not heavy
with the feeling

of letting
someone else
down.

◉

Saguaro cactuses
are taller

and older
than I could
have imagined.

I've never been
to a desert
or to a national park.

Never made room
for it
in my dreams.

Never thought
of it as
something I
could want.

📍

When Eri said
we should
come here,

I imagined
driving
to a destination
of nowhere.

   Trekking to
   an empty field.

Hiking out here
to see nothing.

   But when I
   wander out
   on my own,

   and stand here,
   I see
   miles of
   cactuses

   with arms
   outspread.

Stretching out
to a horizon
dotted with
sharp peaks.

   I spot prickly pear
   flowers,

bright pink,
bursting from
an earth-colored
landscape.

Petals fluttering
in a warm breeze.

For the first time
in my life,

I know quiet.

The peace
of being alone.

Of looking
at myself

with nothing
in the way.

Looking out
over the desert,

I don't find
the nothing
that I thought
was here.

Instead, I find
the parts of me
I'd hidden
away.

♀

Eri is waiting
for me

when I finally
make my way
back to her.

Leaning against
Henrietta.

Dirty
and dusty,

worn hiking
boots crossed
at the ankle.

Shorts baring
dark skin to
a bright
valley sun.

I know
I can do this
with her–

I can go off
on my own

when I need to

and know
she'll be here
when I get back.

I can feel free
to grow
and change,

knowing that
she'll be ready
to face whatever
I bring with me.

      Whatever changes
      may come.

I think she knows
that I'll do
the same
for her.

I call Mom
just before we cross
the border into
California.

It's early
evening back
home, and she's
just left work.

I can hear
cars honking
as she waits
for the bus.

For someone
who planned
every part
of my life,

for someone
who always
seemed to loom
so large,

she sounds
so small

over the static
of the phone.

She asks
if I'm ready
to start classes
in a few days.

If I miss home.

> You're so
> far away
> from me,
> she says.

As if that
wasn't
the point.

I'll feel
bad about that
later.

> For now,
> Eri is wiggling
> into a pair
> of denim shorts.

> Getting ready
> to see
> the Pacific Ocean
> for the first time.

♀

I want to
tell my mom
about Eri.

About the way
she makes me feel

powerful
and loved
and worthy.

The way things
seem to fall
into place
with her beside me.

       About how
       my future is
       less certain.

       About how
       excited
       that makes me.

But maybe,

for now,

I can keep something
just for myself.

PART THREE

A New Home

♀

The Pacific
is colder

than I thought
it would be.

    Shocking
    against warm,
    sunlit sand.

I dig my toes
between grains
of sand.

    Looking for
    what's different.

Searching for
something

that I couldn't
find
back home.

♀

Nearby,
a family

lights a spark.

Drags
driftwood
to a pile as

a fire begins
to roar.

      They see Eri
      and me, sitting
      in the sand
      alone,

      and beckon
      us over.

The afternoon
stretches long

as we laugh
and dance
with strangers.

Free in a way
we've never been.

      Welcomed
      in a way that
      feels new
      and unexpected.

●

I imagine
the fire

burning away
the parts of us

that covered
our true selves
underneath.

       I'll start school
       in a few days–

       the next phase
       of The New Plan,
       the start of
       my future.

Eri
will go back
home–

       back to work
       at her dad's shop.

       Back to a home
       where she must
       answer to
       Maurice.

I think about
what she's
given me–

the chance
to find
the best parts
of me.

The ones
I'd been hiding
from even myself.

Eri sits
beside me,
singing along
to a nearby radio.

Her face seems
to glow in
the low light.

She seems to shine
for the world,
the way she always
has for me.

        I watch
        the sun set
        on the last seconds
        of this day–

        knowing what
        lies ahead.

◉

My heart
begins to twist
at the thought of

leaving Eri alone
at an airport.

       Of seeing her plane
       grow smaller
       and smaller

as it creeps
across the sky.

Of all
the progress
she's made

rewinding
as she inches back
to the East Coast.

       Back to a city,
       back to a home,
       back to a family

       where she'll never
       know peace
       like this again.

I want nothing more
than for her to feel
the way she feels now
every day.

Panic sparks
like a fire in
my chest, and–

      Stay,
      I say.

She turns
to me.

Her dark eyes
are wide.

Anaya?

      Stay here.

Where would we–

      We'll find an apartment.
      I'd sleep in the car
      if it meant you
      wouldn't leave.

But work–

      You can fix a car
      like no one I know.
      Here or anywhere.

But my dad–

      Can't hurt you anymore.

♀

For a moment
I hold my breath.

Afraid she'll say no.

Our hands meet
over grains of
unfamiliar sand.

I ask again.

Eri.
Stay with me.

As if it were
that simple.

Maybe it is.

Eri smiles.

Her fingers
curl around mine.

And she stays.

WANT TO KEEP READING?

If you liked this book, check out another book
from West 44 Books:

Our Broken Earth
By Demitria Lunetta

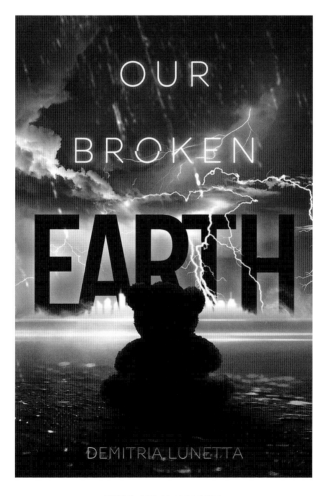

ISBN: 9781978595408

1.

The earth hates us.

With its rising tides
           and poison winds
                   and angry sun
                          and toxic rain.

It's raining now.

None of us dare to brave the storm.

Not for anything.

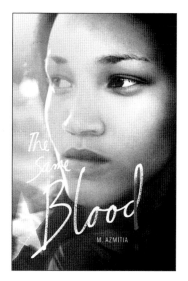

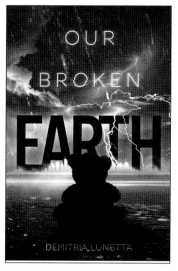

CHECK OUT MORE BOOKS AT:
www.west44books.com

ABOUT THE AUTHOR

M. Azmitia is a government employee by day and a poet/cat lady by night in New York City. She holds a degree in English and creative writing. Azmitia writes about identity, discovery, and acceptance in marginalized communities in the hopes of starting crucial conversations about diversity. Her first novel, *The Same Blood*, is a Junior Library Guild Gold Standard Selection about Latinidad and mental health in families of color.